# The Ghost Dog

## by C. Warren

### illustrated by Pete Smith

**Librarian Reviewer**
Marci Peschke
Librarian, Dallas Independent School District
MA Education Reading Specialist, Stephen F. Austin State University
Learning Resources Endorsement, Texas Women's University

**Reading Consultant**
Mary Evenson
Middle School Teacher, Edina Public Schools, MN
MA in Education, University of Minnesota

**STONE ARCH BOOKS**
Minneapolis   San Diego

First published in the United States in 2008
by Stone Arch Books
151 Good Counsel Drive, P.O. Box 669
Mankato, Minnesota 56002
*www.stonearchbooks.com*

Originally published in Great Britain in 2006
by Badger Publishing Ltd.

*Library of Congress Cataloging-in-Publication Data*
Warren, Celia.
    [Ghost Dog Mystery]
    The Ghost Dog / by C. Warren; illustrated by Pete Smith.
    p. cm. — (Keystone Books)
    Summary: When Nate and Jack move into a new house where they
are awakened during the night by ghostly sounds of a dog howling, they
are led to a starving pup tied up in an abandoned yard.
    ISBN-13: 978-1-59889-847-7 (library binding)
    ISBN-10: 1-59889-847-7 (library binding)
    ISBN-13: 978-1-59889-899-6 (paperback)
    ISBN-10: 1-59889-899-X (paperback)
    [1. Dogs—Fiction. 2. Ghosts—Fiction.] I. Smith, Pete, ill. II. Title.
PZ7.W2515Gh 2008
[Fic]—dc22
                                    2007003166

1 2 3 4 5 6 12 11 10 09 08 07

Printed in the United States of America

# Table of Contents

# Chapter 1

# The First Night

It was the first night in our new house.

My room was full of boxes. They still needed to be unpacked.

"Nate, you will have to sleep in Jack's room," said Dad.

Jack is my brother. I didn't want to sleep in his room.

However, I was glad to be in Jack's room when the noises began.

It was not just the sounds of a new house.

First, there was a howl.

Next, a chain clanking.

When it stopped I held my breath.

But then all of the noises started again: Clank. Howl. Rattle.

"Did you hear anything?" whispered Jack from the other side of the room.

"I heard a clunk, clank noise," I said quietly.

"And a howl," said Jack.

"And a rattle," I said.

Jack sat up in his bed. "Should we see what it is?" he asked.

"I guess so," I said.

We got out of bed and went to
the window.

Neither of us could see anything
outside. What was making the noises?

Another howl made us jump. It
sounded like an animal in pain.

Then there was silence so sudden
that it made me shiver.

Jack was shivering, too.

"Are you scared?" I asked.

"Just cold," he said. "Better go back to bed."

After what seemed like forever, I went back to sleep.

# Chapter 2

# A Buried Bone

Soon, it was morning, and Jack was jumping on my bed.

At first, I was mad at him for waking me up.

I was tired. I had not slept very well the night before.

Jack smiled.

"Nate, come on!" he said. "Let's go explore our new house."

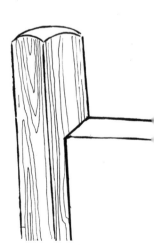

Finally, I climbed out of bed.

I got dressed as fast as I could.

I wanted to explore our new house.

I also wanted to find out what had made those strange, loud noises in the night.

We walked through the house and out the front door.

Then we ran into the back yard. There was nothing in the back that would make a noise.

There was just a post stuck in the ground. It was rusty and bent.

Next to the post, there was some dirt in a big pile.

Jack dug a little in the dirt.

We saw something white. We dug some more. Soon, we found a bone.

"Wow! Do you think there's a body?" I asked.

"No," said Jack. "I think it's an animal bone."

I dug down, looking for more bones.

"Maybe a dog hid it," said Jack. "Dogs do that. Then they come back for them."

"Well, bad luck, doggie!" I said. "I want this bone."

Just then Dad called us. "Nate and Jack! Would you boys please come into the house and help with the boxes?" he said.

Jack ran off like a shot.

I hid the bone quickly. Just in case it belonged to someone.

Or to someone's body, I said to myself.

# Chapter 3

# The White Dog

That night we left the light on in the bedroom, but Dad switched it off.

So it was dark when we woke up later.

The noises had started again.

Jack turned his lamp on.

"Do you think it's foxes?" I said.

"Foxes with chains?" Jack said, shaking his head.

We both got out of our beds and walked to the window.

Then we saw it.

There was a big white dog chained to the rusty post. It was trying to get free.

"Poor dog," I cried.

"Come on," said Jack.

We ran down to the back door.

The dog was still howling.

Jack and I went into the back yard.

The grass was cold and damp on our bare feet.

My hair stood on end as we ran toward the dog.

One second it was there.

The next second it was gone.

I could feel Jack shaking.

I could tell that he was scared. I was scared too.

That dog had disappeared!

"I think it saw us," he said.

Suddenly, the white dog was at the end of the garden.

It looked at us.

Then it ran through a gap in the bushes. Jack and I went after it.

The dog kept running. Sometimes, it stopped and looked at us. Then it gave another howl and ran some more.

Finally, it stopped behind the last house on the street.

The dog looked at us. I couldn't believe it.

We could look right through its thick
white coat and see the fence behind.

Then the dog vanished.

# Chapter 4

# Rescue

Now what could we do?

The white dog was gone. There was nothing else to do, so we started to go home.

Suddenly we heard a sound.

We quickly spun around.

Jack and I peeked through a hole in the fence.

Weeds and long grass grew everywhere.

The yard looked as if it had been forgotten for years.

Then we saw another dog.

It was tied to a tree and lay very still.

This dog was not a ghost. This was a real dog.

It was black and tan. It was so thin we could see its ribs.

"We have to help that dog!" I said.

Jack nodded. His face was pale.

Jack and I ran around to the front of the house.

We banged on the door but the house was empty.

We walked over and checked out the fence that went around the house's yard.

The front gate was locked.

The side gate was broken.

I gave the side gate one hard shake
and it opened.

We raced over to the dog.

The poor thing was trying to drink from the wet grass. It was almost too weak to stand.

If we left it there, we knew it would die. So we carried the dog home to our new house.

# Chapter 5

# A New Friend

Dad was in the kitchen making coffee when Jack, the dog, and I ran through the door.

Dad stood and stared at us with his mouth open.

He was looking at Jack and me and the sad dog.

Dad loves dogs. He had one when he was a boy, but has not had one since then.

He put his coffee cup down to pet
the dog right away.

"Where did you find this dog?"
Dad asked.

Jack and I looked at each other.

"He was tied up at an empty house
down the street," Jack told Dad.

Dad asked, "How did you know to
look for him there?"

I didn't know how to explain that a ghost dog had led us to the sick dog.

Dad fed the dog some ham. It licked his hand.

"Boys, I think we should take this dog to a vet," Dad said. "I think he's sick. It looks like he has been starving."

Later that morning, we all piled into the car and took the dog to the vet's office in town.

The vet looked at the dog's paws, ears, and teeth.

"You poor thing!" she said. "You are all skin and bones. But these boys found you in time. You are lucky."

The vet smiled. "He's very young," she told us.

She looked at Jack and me. "If you two feed him well and keep him warm, he should be okay. It shouldn't take long to get him strong again."

The vet gave the dog a shot to make sure that it wouldn't get sick.

Then we took the dog home.

# Chapter 6

# Lucky

Dad made some phone calls about the dog, but no one was missing one. So he said we could keep the dog.

We chose a name. We would call our dog "Lucky."

A week later I remembered the bone. I stepped into the back yard to go look for it.

Then we saw Lucky digging by the rusty post.

He had dug up the bone in the very same place as we did! Lucky lay down, licking his bone happily.

We never saw the big white dog again. But our new neighbor, the man next door, smiled when we asked him.

"The people who lived here before had a rescue dog. Snowy, they called him. He used to lie in the yard licking his bone. Just like Lucky!"

# About the Author

Celia Warren has written numerous stories and poems for young people, many of which have been broadcast on television and radio. Some of her poems have even been set to music. She lives in Devon, England.

# Glossary

**chain** (CHAYN)—a series of metal rings joined together

**explore** (ek-SPLOR)—to travel around to find out what a place is like

**forgotten** (for-GOT-in)—not remembered

**gap** (GAP)—a space between things

**post** (POHST)—a long, thick piece of wood or metal that is stuck in the ground to support or mark something

**ribs** (RIBZ)—the long, curved bones that support your chest and protect your heart and lungs

**vanished** (VAN-ishd)—disappeared

# Discussion Questions

1. Have you ever found a sick animal? What did you do to help it?

2. Have you ever moved into a new house? What are some things that are hard about moving? What are some things that are fun?

3. Can you explain the big white dog that the brothers saw? Why did it appear?

# Writing Prompts

1. In this book, the ghost dog was helping the poor dog who had been abandoned. What if the ghost came back? Do you think it would help another pet or animal? Pretend you are Nate or Jack and the ghost dog comes back a second time. Write what happens next.

2. Do you have a pet? If you don't, would you like to have one? What kind of pet would it be? What would you name it? Write about all the good things about having your pet.

3. Do you believe in ghosts? Why or why not? Write your reasons.

# If You Liked This Book . . .

### Sleepwalker
*by J. Powell*

*When Josh decides to follow
Tom one night on one of his
sleepwalking adventures,
real life suddenly turns into
a nightmare!*

### 5010 Calling
*by J. Powell*

*The year is 5010. Beta sets up
a thought-link with Zac from
the year 2000 to help with his
history project. Zac doesn't mind
helping out with the homework,
until Beta gets him into trouble!*

# . . . You'll Love These!

### Steel Eyes
*by Jonny Zucker*

*Emma Stone is the new girl in school. Why does she always wear sunglasses? Gail and Tanya are determined to find out, but Emma's cold stare is more than they bargained for.*

### Space Games
*by David Orme*

*Todd's travels across the universe are no match for a good game of soccer. When a soccer field is built aboard his starship, he dreams of leading his team to universal glory.*

# Internet Sites

Do you want to know more about subjects related to this book? Or are you interested in learning about other topics? Then check out FactHound, a fun, easy way to find Internet sites.

Our investigative staff has already sniffed out great sites for you!

Here's how to use FactHound:

1. Visit *www.facthound.com*

2. Select your grade level.

3. To learn more about subjects related to this book, type in the book's ISBN number: **1598898477**.

4. Click the **Fetch It** button.

FactHound will fetch the best Internet sites for you!